WHERE IS GAH-NING?

STORY BY
ROBERT MUNSCH

ILLUSTRATED BY
HÉLÈNE DESPUTEAUX

ANNICK PRESS LTD.
TORONTO • NEW YORK

One day Gah-Ning went to her father
and said, "I want to go on a trip."
Her father stopped working and said,
"Oh, are you going to go to a movie?"
"No," said Gah-Ning.
"Going to go to a hockey game?"
"No," said Gah-Ning.
"Going to the store?"
"No," said Gah-Ning.
"Well, where are you going?" asked her father.
"I," said Gah-Ning, "am going to go
to Kapuskasing."

"No," said her father. "I know about Kapuskasing. When people go to Kapuskasing they spend hundreds of dollars. They shop and shop and shop and spend all their money."

"I want to go to Kapuskasing anyway!" said Gah-Ning.

"No way," said her father.

Gah-Ning sat on the front steps of the restaurant for a while. Then she got her bicycle and started pedalling down the road to Kapuskasing.

When it was lunch time, the father said, "Where is Gah-Ning?"

"I don't know," said her mother. "The last time I saw her, she was going down the street on her bicycle."

"On her bicycle?" said her father.

"Gah-Ning?"

"Bicycle!"

"Kapuskasing!!!"

"Oh, no!!!!!"

He jumped into their car and started driving down the road. He drove almost halfway to Kapuskasing and there was Gah-Ning, pedalling like crazy. The father stopped and said, "What's the matter with you? Are you crazy? There are trucks. There are cars. There are buses. There are motorcycles. You're going to get killed!"

He picked up the bicycle and threw it
in the trunk. When they got home Gah-Ning's
father looked at her and said, "Don't
drive your bicycle to Kapuskasing."
Then he went back to the restaurant and
started making chicken balls.
Gah-Ning sat on the front steps for a while,
and then went to get her roller blades.

When it was time for dinner, her father said, "Where is Gah-Ning?"

"I don't know," said her mother. "The last time I saw her she was going down the road on her roller blades."

"Roller blades?" said the father.

"Gah-Ning?"

"Roller blades!"

"Kapuskasing!!!"

"Oh, no!!!!!"

He jumped into the car and drove down the road to Kapuskasing. About fifty kilometres out of town, there was Gah-Ning, skating along.

The father stopped and said, "What's the matter with you? Are you crazy? There are trucks. There are cars. There are buses. There are motorcycles! You are going to get killed!

"Don't go to Kapuskasing on your bicycle. Don't go to Kapuskasing on a bus. Don't go to Kapuskasing on a skateboard and don't go to Kapuskasing in a helicopter. Just don't go!"

The next day, Gah-Ning got up and said, "Oh, here I am and I really want to take a trip."
But since she couldn't go out of town, she went downtown to the library. There she met a clown who was doing a show for kids. At the end of his performance he gave out balloons.

He said to the first kid, "How many balloons do you want?"
The kid said, "Two balloons."
He said to the second kid, "How many balloons do you want?"
The kid said, "One balloon."
Gah-Ning came up and the clown said, "How many balloons do you want?"
Gah-Ning said, "Three hundred."
"Three hundred balloons!!!" said the clown. "I never gave anyone that many before."

So he gave Gah-Ning one hundred balloons, two hundred balloons, three hundred balloons, and Gah-Ning started to float right up into the sky. The clown said, "You'd better look out. You are going to float all the way to Kapuskasing."

"I know," said Gah-Ning, "isn't it great?"

When it was lunch time, her father said, "Where is Gah-Ning?"
"I don't know," said her mother. "She went to the library and she hasn't come back."
Her father walked down to the library and said, "Where is my kid?"

"Oh," said the librarian, "so that was your kid. She's on her way to Kapuskasing."

"Oh, no," said her father. "Is she on a bicycle?"

"No," said the librarian.

"Is she on roller blades?"

"No," said the librarian.

"Then how is she getting to Kapuskasing?" asked the father.

"With three hundred balloons," said the librarian. "She is floating down the Trans-Canada Highway holding onto three hundred balloons."

"Oh, no!!!" yelled the father.

He jumped into the car, drove all the way to Kapuskasing and parked by a shopping mall. He looked up, and there was Gah-Ning coming down out of the sky, letting go of one balloon at a time. She came down right on top of her father's car. Gah-Ning looked at him and said, "Daddy! You came to go shopping. How nice!

"And you brought little sister, too."

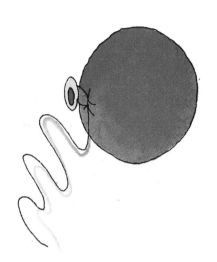

about this story

This book started with a letter. It was from Gah-Ning, who lived in a little town in Northern Ontario. On the back of her letter she had drawn a wonderful picture of a girl going up in a balloon. I liked the picture so much that I wrote a not-very-good story about it and sent it to her. Gah-Ning must have liked the story, because she kept writing me lots of letters.

A year later I decided that it would be neat to meet her, so I flew up north and told stories at her school. She asked me to tell everyone the story I had sent her in the mail, so I told it, but it changed a lot and turned into a really-very-good story. As soon as I told it I knew that it would be a book someday.

When I was done, Gah-Ning said, "My sister, Fone-Ning, and I want to show you the most important things in town. The very most important things." They started with the Chinese restaurant.

"This," said Gah-Ning, "is our uncle's restaurant. It has the best chicken balls in Canada! We make them ourselves. Everybody else uses frozen chicken balls. Ours are the best."
"The best in Canada???" I asked.
"He doesn't believe us," whispered Fone-Ning.
"He probably couldn't tell a chicken ball from a baseball," whispered Gah-Ning.

Then we walked and walked till we came to a toy store. Fone-Ning said, "Look, toys. Kids' toys. This is a very important thing in town. Everybody comes here. If the toys weren't here, nobody would even live here." Then they rode toy cars up and down the aisles until a lady yelled at them in French.
"What's she saying?" I asked.
"She says we have to go," said Gah-Ning.
"Maybe that was the most important thing in town?" I asked.

"No, no," said the girls. "This is not the most important thing in town. We haven't even seen the moose yet."
"Moose?" I said.
"Definitely a moose," they said.

We walked for a long time and finally, on the edge of town, we came to a very large statue of a moose.
"Look at that," I said. "A moose! I can see why that is the most important thing in town. Not every town has an enormous statue of a moose. In fact, most towns don't even have a small statue of a moose."
"No," said Fone-Ning. "The moose is important, but it's not the most important thing in town. We haven't even been to the most important thing in town."
"What's that?" I asked.

Then we walked over some railroad tracks, through some deep snow, and through some bushes and finally came out on a dirt road that was full of trucks carrying logs. We kept going and finally, way out in the middle of noplace, we came to a field. There, sticking out of the snow, were gravestones.
"A cemetery?" I asked.
"This is where our grandmother is buried," said Gah-Ning.
Both sisters stood in the blowing snow and bowed to the grave. When they were done I asked, "Why did you do that?"
"That," said Fone-Ning, "is what you do when you go visit your grandmother's grave."
"Right," I said. "This wouldn't happen to be the most important thing in town?"
"Absolutely," said Gah-Ning.
"No doubt about it," said Fone-Ning.

Then we walked all the way back to the restaurant. It was dark and really cold. When we got back I was so cold I could only eat five chicken balls, and that was too bad, because they really were the best chicken balls in Canada.

Bob Munsch

to Gah-Ning and Fone-Ning Tang,
Hearst, Ontario — R.M.

to Delphine — H.D.

©1994 Bob Munsch Enterprises Ltd. (text)
©1994 Hélène Desputeaux (art)
Design by Michel Aubin

Annick Press Ltd.

Annick Press gratefully acknowledges the support of the Canada
Council and the Ontario Arts Council.

Canadian Cataloguing in Publication Data

Munsch, Robert N., 1945-
    Where is Gah Ning?

(Munsch for Kids)
ISBN 1-55037-983-6 (bound) ISBN 1-55037-982-8 (pbk.)

I. Desputeaux, Hélène. II. Title. III. Series:
Munsch, Robert N., 1945-   . Munsch for kids.

PS8576.U67W53 1994   jC813'.54   C94-930734-3
PZ7.M86Wh 1994

Distributed in Canada by: Published in the U.S.A. by Annick Press (U.S.) Ltd.
Firefly Books Ltd.   Distributed in the U.S.A. by:
250 Sparks Ave.   Firefly Books (U.S.) Inc.
Willowdale, ON M2H 2S4   P.O. Box 1338
                                   Ellicott Station
                                   Buffalo, NY 14205

Printed and bound in Canada by
Metropole Litho, Quebec